"what do i mean to you?",

she asked.

"the world."

...he thought to himself.

this side up

an incomplete collection of mostly poetry

by Lian Waite

Because It's Thursday Publishing
2019

www.becauseitsthursday.com

First Printing: 76, G
ISBN 978-0-9966837-9-1

Written, edited & arranged by Lian Waite
All photography & artwork by Lian Waite unless otherwise noted.

This book contains material from
Bare With Me, I'm Terrible With Names (© 2015) by Lian Waite.

Because It's Thursday Publishing
www.becauseitsthursday.com
To contact the author email robert@becauseitsthursday.com

to everyone that has been to our acre of "The Creek."

Dear Reader,

Please take your time.
Read a poem.
Close the book.
Take a break.
Take your time with these words.
They may not be the best, but they're mine...
Well, they were.
Now they're yours, please be gentle.

I hope you find something that you can enjoy.
I hope you find something that means something to you.
I hope you can find something that you understand.

I left a few writings unfinished.
Hopefully you can understand this process.
Hopefully you can forgive me.

Maybe you'll love these words.
Maybe you'll hate these words.
I appreciate either.
Please.
Proceed with caution.

Thank you, enjoy.
LW

i live a building of 18 floors.

The first floor has a twelve-foot high by twelve-foot wide revolving door with no lock and 30 foot high ceilings. The front wall is floor to ceiling glass and the room itself is shaped like a triangle so that you can see the two other walls even before you enter the room. Those walls have custom wallpaper covered with a seemingly infinite amount of jokes, funny comments, and quips about life and my surroundings. The first floor has no elevator, and all stairways are guarded by security, access is invite only.

The second floor is an ever playing karaoke band.

The third floor is a four foot and two-inch deep swimming pool. There are only three walls on the third floor, and from the open wall you can see out and across the street into a neighboring apartment which is over a restaurant. There is a slide that descends from a higher floor into the pool. The family in the apartment across the street has a black lab named Lady.

The fourth floor is a soundproof and padded room with no windows and no doors, only a desk with a self-powering lamp and a chair. On the desk is a single notebook turned to the fourth page, which is blank, and the cursor blinking frantically as if begging to be sped along the page chasing thought and leaving a trail of mystical beauty.

The fifth floor is silent. The only tenant listens intently to the floor with a stethoscope trying to decipher what is going on below him.

The sixth floor is a telescope and just high enough to see over all the buildings in the neighborhood. In the distance, you can see a great bonfire where men stand around warming themselves in the winter weather.

The seventh floor has a glass ceiling, and the eighth has a glass floor, and all the tenants dance nude in the rain and share stories about love when they knew it at it's most innocent.

The ninth floor is a church. A synagogue. A mosque. A temple. A holy place. A refuge. A sanctuary. There is no elevator stop on the ninth floor and the stairs are a separate staircase that lead directly from the ground floor.

The tenth floor is a drug-induced, party of a lifetime extravaganza sponsored by Red Bull, Tito's Vodka and your neighborhood drug dealer.

The eleventh floor is a rainstorm because "a man ain't supposed to cry."

The twelfth floor is a giant slip n slide that goes into a tunneled slide out of the window. Don't worry, you'll be dropped off below.

Here is where I store names.

The fourteenth floor is filled with books. Bursting at the seams with knowledge. The fourteenth floor is goddamned special and if you don't know about it, this is where you'd go to find out.

The fifteenth floor has a better view of that bonfire and from here you can see the burning homes of a neighboring village and the cannibalistic nature of the men feasting, over a roaring fire, on the carcasses of its prior inhabitants.

The sixteenth floor is a speeding car tearing through the countryside at literal break-neck speeds on a warm fall afternoon. With so many leaves flying through the air it's a wonder you don't lose your way down the road from watching them in the rearview. Shift up to 5th gear, step on the gas young man, don't take heed to the warning signs, take that curve as fast as you can...die if you must.

The seventeenth floor has 9,000 rooms and only one has a bed. I couldn't guess to tell you which room has that bed because there are hired servants whose only job is to move that bed around constantly between the rooms. Their only instruction is to never let me find it no matter how hard I search...I may never get to rest.

The eighteenth floor is where the woman I love the most lives. Her skin, so beautiful, so pure, so magnificently perfect, despite what the world tries to make her believe. She sleeps in each of the 25 rooms with her own personal security outside of the door. She tells a story with her steps and writes a movie with her glance. She is my wife. She is my sister. She is my mother. She is my daughter. She is my aunt. She is my neighbor. She has a son and I protect him as well.

-eight words

"make sure that whenever you smile, it's honest."

-tsp.

   If you ever have the chance to swim in a thought, never pass
that up...never. But always know that
everything doesn't have to have the deepest meaning.

   Everything doesn't have to be like the ocean.

   Sometimes you want to let whatever it is be just what it is.

   A hand to touch.

   A gust of wind.

   Sometimes i just want her to rest her hand on my back until i
fall asleep. Some moments only call for a teaspoon worth and in
that moment the best tool is just that, a teaspoon.

i can smell her perfume when the wind blows just right.
...never really been a gambling man.
she likes sunflowers, i know this because i care.
finding something to have is good, finding her was better.
at least where I sit I'm doing okay.
if she loved me enough to fill the little pocket on my jeans,
that'd be enough really.
i treat her good, she treats me better.
...I can live with that.

-try and stop me

Teach me to fall.
I'm tired.
I'm so tired of holding on and I just wish to learn to let go.
Tired of fighting on my own and I'm starting to feel weak.
Show me how to love you.
Teach me about you. Let me learn.
Teach me to care.

Teach me the best way to your heart.

Show me how to love you.

Then try your best to stop me.

-appendages

fingers & toes and
fingers and toes &
fingers n toes they keep us going.
her little fingers know toes and
her fingers, nose, toes
know toes like mine that love her.

-brain matter

i see Cupid's got a gun
shooting bullets at the sun
won't you waste some on me...

won't choose 'cides, cause this is love.
just make sure the deed is done,
don't you leave me lonely.

-waiting for this photo to save

raw files take up so much space..
after the pizza place that i took you to,
something said i might be spending a bit more time with you.
do you remember that gay bar that we walked into?
and you shot pool just as good as i do.
well...almost.   ——

that was when I met Dumb Sister...
she's not so sure how far a mile really is.

it's still kinda warm in October here,
maybe that's why you stayed...

I'll probably never learn how to make coffee.
Even if I don't like how yours taste, I wouldn't say.
I like that you share that with me.

I'm just waiting for this photo to save then I'll be on my way to
you.

-i'm so sorry

i'm so sorry...
...if sometimes you think that you're anything less than amazing.
...if you think you're anything less than magic.
...if you've ever thought you were anything less than beautiful.

i'm so sorry...
...that you'll never have a hurricane named after you.
there may be storms with the same name, but they'll never be
named after you...
hurricanes are powerful, beautifully destructive forces of nature,
just like your love
but you can predict them, you can see them coming, you can
prepare for hurricanes.
you gave me no chance to prepare for you. there was no way i
could see this coming.

i'm so sorry...
...about the blood on my sleeve.

i'm so sorry...
...that you'll never get to make love to another.

i'm so sorry...
that i never explained the ankle weights.
it's because I still float like a dream every time you tell me you
love me.

i'm so sorry...
if I don't challenge you enough, I'm still working on me.

-"...addressed to Jane Doe"

Dearest Jane,

Thank you for being You. Beautiful. Majestic. Perfectly imperfect in your own many ways and in all of your many forms. Just know that God, whatever your God may be, dreams nightly to wake and create daily and He has done this over 108 billion times still somehow managing to have enough beauty left over when he made you to render me speechless. You are powerful. You are chosen by that same God to be the vessel through which life is created, that in itself is a feat worth much praise. You are this world and it would not exist without you. Your glow is what lights the morning sky and the peace of your mind is what allows me to sleep at night. You are special. With thoughts deep enough to swim in and a smile bright enough to blind ten generations, you are love personified. I see your ambition. I see your determination. You are proud and rightfully so. Remember each time you fall that it is your will and not your legs that power you to keep going, so keep going and never give up. Never give up, no matter what, because your sister is counting on you. Your sister and your brother too, we need you more than you might imagine. Again I beg of you, never conform and always be true. There's only one you and there can never be two. Cry when you need to and smile when you wish just to remind the world how lucky it really is... to have you, to know you. Love your sister, because you know her struggle. Love me, because you know how much I need it. Love the world, because through you is the only way it can truly be healed. There haven't been words created that can accurately express my full admiration for you, but this is as close as I can manage. Thank you Jane and God bless you.

-your last.

-vicodin

...when I see other women dressed sexy I find myself imagining how it would look on her. maybe today it's because the dentist has me on vicodin...maybe I love her.

Who knows

-Human Nature

today I realized that I hate the sun
for the way it kisses your skin.
and for the way it plays in your hair,
I don't get along with the wind.
Every sight that steals your gaze,
just puts me in a haze.
...and because you love to sleep with it,
I just can't stand the rain.

-party bruises

...an idle mind is a dangerous place to be in,
open your eyes and mind then tune your ears and heart and
believe me.

you see, you never really stood a chance.
you started with a disadvantage.
somehow you dropped from your clouds
to fall to me through the trees
and I was already down on my knees
ready to catch you...

cuts to your pride and a bruise on your knee...
I've taken hits to the gut and might be missing some teeth
but nevertheless just keep your faith in me
and let me lead you to a better place
right where we need to be..

lean on me if you need a brace, I'll try to walk at an even pace
I see no need to race.

let me ask you...would you leave it?
all, except the shoes on your feet

would you bet it all on me?

-lucky me

funny thing to me, I can't picture her face.
fingers, legs, toes, hips, breasts...all there,
but I can't picture her face.
we're still pretty new so I guess it's fine. I mean I've
only kissed her a couple hundred times.
I enjoy this though. I find a twisted pleasure in it.
I'm trying like shit to picture her face. I feel like it makes me
think
of her more, it makes me want her closer.
I want to see her now. I want to see how close I got with the
picture I created.
I won't look at a photo, that'd be too much like cheating the game.
I get to look at her like it's my first time, every time...
imagine that.
I know one day I'll be able to picture her face all the time.
I'm looking forward to that day too.
Lucky me.

"I know I'm in denial, but it won't take a whole day to explain to you why I smile."

-Friday, February 10, 2017. 1:17 am

my last conversation each day is when I speak to God about her.

my last conversation with her was last week.

...she says I don't text enough.

...now i just have the bittersweet memories of a life that i once knew. if i had it to do again i'd do it all the same. i miss it. i miss her...but as it turns out, she missed something a bit more real.

she needed something concrete. something she could punch. something she could lay a hand to.

this wife that i had didn't dream of movie night with the girls and dinner time with the kids.

this wife i had needed something she could taste.

trust me, i asked questions too...but she told me that I was a sound in a world full of flavors and she didn't have the heart anymore to do me any favors.

When i asked her my tune she said that i was blue and that she yearned for a new taste even though i was a sight too.

each word. each word she used...she used it today, and today... today was the best day to be in love. the best day for us.

I'm a married man...still on the up and up. Still trying to keep my wife happy. still committed.

but I'm afraid I'm losing it, the spark, the fire, the flame.

I have no idea how to do this, but today isn't the day for doubt.

there's no way i'm ever letting her go. She smiles at me smiling at her right back still.

even after this many years. and there's so much truth in her smile. so much life.

so much effort in her heart, so much thought.

Her long nightly rituals remind me of love. Face lotion, body lotion, hand lotion, foot lotion.

Nightly rituals. I look forward to nightly rituals. I don't want to miss this.

I dream her and she dreams me...that's the language we speak in our sleep...

I mean what else do you expect from a couple of newlyweds?

Last night she spoke from her heart and I got lost in her thoughts...I swam for hours in deep conversation with the love of my life. My forever. My tomorrow and the day after.

what an eloquent tongue, what a soothing mind. what a lucky fucking guy I must be to land someone so beautiful, so perfect.

I have a wife now and I know it'll all be worth it.

I mean, I know it's gonna be work once we're married, but we've been engaged for a while...we've lived together too.

I'll have a Wife once we get to the big day. I'm excited, i'm so nervous, I'm so ready.

I'm almost done writing my vows...it's going to be perfect. She's gonna love it.

I'm better at picturing her face, lucky me...

...I can't wait to see her face when I pop the question.

I think it's time. I think I'm ready, I hope she is too...this feeling is crazy.

I....me.....we're made for each other...right? Yea...it's gonna be awesome...and even if it doesn't
work out and if I had to do it again I'd do it all the same...
sometimes I miss her, but I know that's
about to change...I'll never have to miss her again.

I'm so excited...I think I found the girl of my dreams and today is our first date.

Damn, we've been talking for weeks...weeks and weeks and an eternity it feels like. But it's
finally happening. I think I found a good one. Maybe it'll turn into something, but who knows?

Almost time to get dressed...I can't wait to show her to my friends...but what do I say?

Hey...let me introduce you to a girl I just met, a very new friend of mine...

-two words

effort + action

-how do you know?

let's say your favorite food is pizza. i say let's order pizza from anywhere you like, i'm buying. you already know where you want to order from because you know which pizza you like best. you know you've had bad pizza from some places and you've had enough pizzas in your lifetime to know when you've found a winner. you know you'd pick that one every time, even subconsciously...it's kinda like that.

-rotten eggs

you know how you say "last one to the car is a rotten egg..." then
you race? well even though i know i'm faster, that first and second
step i have to really try or she might win this time...
she laughs, I laugh. that counts.

-"Is It Me?"

sometimes I want to write about you.
'cause I keep finding so many things right about you.
poor timing has us hiding field trips from kinship
as feelings grow more intrinsic to our friendship.
in plain sight I try to keep you in my minds eye
'cause eyes spy when I'd spy you under moonlight.
that dress kissing on your skin, dancing 'round your curves
you do bad so good and I'm just trying to learn.
catch myself dreaming 'bout that body, mostly in the day.
heels on and them legs seem to go for days.
we sneak glances and that ass has me in a daze,
you blow me kisses on the sly sending me in a craze.
is it me or is this room getting hot as shit?
i'll cool off in your kiss, but keep it tight-lipped.
you text and tell me how you're lonely, longing for my touch
but you know problems get started when you start to rush...
...shhhh.

to date, this is the second best collection of words that I have had the opportunity of putting together in the form of a single poem.

the first was written as a draft on Facebook, it got deleted somehow…

this one is for the girl that thinks she weighs too much for her height and fights the fight to make her shorter than average legs climb the stairs at night.

if you have ever had a conversation in the dark with God until you began to sweat tears because you believe that there is someone or something up there bigger than us all, I wrote this for you.

…and if you have not.

these words are for my black friends that understand privilege.

…and for my white friends that don't.

this is for the girl, that's gay, black and just enough of a Muslim trying to make her way in America.

this is for the college kids rioting in the streets looking for a revolution and legalized marijuana and for the quiet protesters that don't have a parallel to that but they fight anyway.

I write this for the eighteen-year-old newly-wed girl who is about to spend her first night away from home with her one-day abusive husband. Know that the world has not forgotten about you, even after he has gone, remember how strong your will has become.

this is for the eleven-year-old boy with the jeans that fit perfect last year but just didn't seem to grow as fast as he did, wearing sneakers that are a quarter size too big so they flop off his feet.

this is for the boy that, just like me, is terrified to speak in public.

this is for the girl that eats caviar on a stale cracker.

(this has been intentionally left unfinished and will be continued.)

"There is religion in solitude, and also where the most beautifully wild things are kept."

Let me write you a song that you can hum all day and poems that
you can keep on your heart like sticky notes.

I know you're ticklish on your toes and tender on your heart.
I know that you hunger for knowledge,
so let's go on a day date and learn something new together.

I'm done growing taller so help me expand my mind, I'm so
intrigued by what I don't know.

Have you ever seen the Northern Lights in person? I haven't.

I know, I know...I'm all over the place, but I mean well.
In the end I can't promise much more than honesty, effort and a
few smiles, so I hope that's enough to start.

...her hair, a crown full of curls that appear to cascade from the heavens, tongue kissed, twisted and tightened by the sun while being styled by the westward winds of the winter weather.

her skin, still every perfect shaded earth-toned hue, with eyes that burn bright like illuminated jades that reflect to me the troubles of a world far, far lost.

I see your heart little fair skinned girl. I made these words for you. I heard twice your thoughts little fair skinned girl. You made these words for you.

...and then they ask, because they always do, what the mixture is that makes you. they always tend to ask the deepest question but use the most shallow words and you wonder "how can you fit the ocean in a teaspoon?"

with the sincerest naivety they create words that seem to simmer from the bottom of their hearts. words that soar to the top of their lungs and when they reach the roofs of their mouths they have a tendency to roll off their tongues to ask you what they think is simply..."what are you mixed with?"

yes little fair skinned girl, just what are you mixed with?

the question resonates through her entire existence. through her ears and into her bones, down her spine and shaking the very foundation that she stands upon.

as shallow as the sea and as meaningless as a Selma, Alabama bus seat...at least to her. commonplace, yes. unwarranted, yes. unwelcome, yes. unanswered, no...

with an expectant half-sigh that turns into just a grand inhale to be able to expel her reply...

"as you can see, I am a little fair skinned girl..." she replies, "...and I am mixed with love and hate. enough blood produced daily that I could quite possibly flood the banks of the great Mississippi River. hope, hurt and great ambition. bones and stardust that has come together to form flesh that will heal over every cut placed upon it. I am mixed with the great silence of the night and too many words because I have a lot to say. a smile that brightens someone's day and an attitude that gets me into trouble..."

"...you want to know what I'm mixed with?" she asks. "I'll let you know exactly what was dropped in the mold when I was created, because oh yes, I am a grand concoction of a creation."...

(this has been intentionally left unfinished and will be continued.)

Dear Reader,

the text on the following page is a small collection of notes for a
poem that I was writing for my mother.

unfortunately, I was not able to share this with her before her
passing, but I am choosing to leave it just as it is, including the
blank pages that follow it.

Verdine Urquhart
1945 (lived & loved) 2019

thank you.

-class of 2003

shake the dust Wa
ww2
19th amendment
that baby's smile calmed the world I'm talking World War 2,
A rose born in a firestorm, the light in my world's war too.
This is a flower for the cleaner and I hope by it's finish you'll be
able to accept it.
Accept it in all it's glory and all it's mystique.
Accept it in all it's great absences and all that it encompasses.

what did you want to grow up to be? i still want to be like you.

you have always been the sunrise that shows up after every one of
my darkest nights
I remember a day or so after my grandma died that it registered
to me that my mother just lost her mother.

(this has been intentionally left unfinished and will be continued.)

-caviar on a stale cracker

I've written a novel and a symphony for her, but she only knows about the poems. Even then she's only heard the ones that I can actually fathom to speak.
So many conversations with God about her that I at times forget my own name. Speaking of names, little does she know that hers has spent so much time on my tongue that I haven't been able to taste food in weeks.

who does God pray to? whoever it is

if you believe in a God, know that we all came from the same one.

 I hope she knows that I look to her for approval.

(this has been intentionally left unfinished and will be continued.)

Dear Reader,

in 2017, I participated in a life changing
peronal and career building
program that my employer sponsored.

the very first assignment was to write your own eulogy.

the text on the following page is what I wrote as my eulogy and
I'm just hoping to come close.

for sake of clarification, my given name is Robert Urquhart Jr.

thank you.

-#goals

Robert Urquhart Jr, a man of many hats. He was a son, husband, father, brother and a real friend. He was also a writer, business owner, mechanic, genius, contractor, football player, chef and a comedian. He often said "people do it all the time, right", whenever he was tasked to try something that he may not have been familiar with. He thought that he could do anything.

If you asked anyone close to him they'd say he loved his family, football and pizza and in no particular order.

I never saw him angry. The few times I did see him get upset, it didn't last long and it was more disappointment than anger. He had no problem telling you the honest thing even if it wasn't the popular thing to say and any time he ever gave me bad advice he stood right beside me and walked through it with me.

Money was no issue, but we're not here to talk about money beeause that wasn't his focus. Life is about how you make people feel and Robert made people feel good, feel appreciated, feel special. He was the type to go chat with the quiet person in the corner just to make sure everyone felt included. He was friends to everybody and anybody. He was my friend and I will forever miss him.

-gifted

"i'm just unwrapping this shaky present, hoping to leave a perfect past."

-quiet zesting juxtaposition

       In the English language we use only 26 letters, but you get to make so many words....and you can throw those words together and use those words to make so many combinations of sounds called sentences. 26 letters constructed and arranged then deconstructed and rearranged to create a different word where resting on each syllable is the greatest potential. there is so much potential in these 26 letters... hell, some of them rarely even get used. how fuckin sick is that? when was the last time you used Q, Z, J or an X? I'm wearing a denim shirt, sitting in a restaurant waiting on eggs benedict. Eggs Benedict...

written in sans and translated to my tongue by stone
these letters forged during the midday light of New Delhi,
written by the star light of the New York sky.
these letters, these words that mean but do not feel.
words that do more than heal...
I've learned that letters, when rearranged, teach.
only 26, but I've had them moved and twisted
contorted and formed enough that I've learned.
each ounce of this blood in my veins is a miracle.
i've taken so many days for granted.
i've learned with these words in what language a baby must
dream.

and

(this has been intentionally left unfinished and will be continued.)

-there's a good chance that none of this matters in the end

yesterday i had two separate dreams about white tigers.

one tiger was nice like a puppy...apparently this is a bad omen.

this morning, just a second before I woke, in my dream someone
said about me...

"he's just laying there like a piece of soap."

...Sara turned off the alarm.

I presume somewhere there is a happy medium...

maybe it's acrylic on canvas so that the cloth won't break down.

it's probably a photograph or a poem.

-(handclap + pancakes)

i immediately catch myself giving more thought into a title for
this than content.

i'm forcing quite a bit currently... funny part is how much of that
is poetic. so profound. so reflective.

Frank sings

(i'd like to leave most of it all behind)

...but i'm def not brave.

would it be easier to make $1,000,000 1 time or make $1 one
million times?

(she's teaching me about me right now)

Frank sings softly

this is not my story. this is ours. this is an interpolation...make
this your own.

i call bullshit. poetry. it's bullshit. all of it.

maybe not the work itself, but in having to label that work as
poetry.

once it's labeled then it's compared.

should I be compared to Voltaire?

or is that the beauty in it?

i can be compared to Voltaire.

-nine words

be someone's somebody.

even if it's only your own.

"...and I feel like that's okay really.

When I was eleven, early 1997, I didn't have a dream job but I did still have a favorite color and that color was blue. Now I work a job that didn't even exist then and I just find comfort in any sight that makes me feel something.

Make me feel something, please.

That was an honest request...of you.

My father died that year, of natural causes.

Make me feel something, because for years all I felt inside is blue.

The death-grip like hold of self-diagnosed and self-treated depression held my hand and walked with me for many years. Skipping and prancing, dancing and smiling. Blue.

There was not one particular event that sent me down the road to despair, but more so a small truckload of things that I had not yet learned to control and file away as they were meant to be disposed of internally.

The day before he died we had cake and ice cream with my mom, his mom and his sisters. That was a novelty.

I don't remember being sad when I was eleven. I do remember not making the honor roll though, because that weighed more than being sad then.

...and I feel like that's okay really.

What a mad mix of a teenager I must have been, huh? Kudos to my mother, she never gave up on me.

She was always proud of me...always. I do remember my mother being proud of me and that weighs more than being sad.

...I'm sure we can all agree that that's okay really.

I remember sitting on the futon in my one bedroom apartment in 2011 glaring out of a slightly cracked door out into nothingness. A world full of nothing, well something, but nothing that I had taken a part in creating.

I remember crying once, for hours uncontrollably, wishing I could figure out this thing called life.

I drank heavily for about 200 days of 2009.

I remember a conversation with myself years later because I wasn't where I thought I'd be in life. I couldn't name one thing that I felt was an accomplishment. In that conversation I talked about dying. I never actually wanted to hurt myself, but I did consider what the best option would be if I had to do it myself. I guess you could say that I weighed the pros and cons of suicide.

That's such an ugly word...but its truth and truth isn't always attractive.

I do remember that beautiful summer breeze blowing over my face, kissing and flirting with me as I wondered how I would end it all if I did decide to do it and that caused me to cry.

...and I feel like that's not okay really.

When I was twenty-five I felt that my biggest accomplishment was that I hadn't died yet.

...that I hadn't died yet, yea...that was the best thing I felt that I had ever done.

I think that was about as low as I made it.

I feel like that was low enough for me.

I think the saddest part of being in a hole that dark is that you think nobody cares but you'd be surprised at who really does.

Having an idea of what it's like makes you wish that you could take those feelings and lock them away. Somewhere so far that water couldn't reach and forgetfulness didn't even visit. You don't want anyone else to feel that way so you find a reason to smile, even if it's just to brighten someone else's day.

I'm thirty and a few years old today and I'm not dead yet...still my biggest accomplishment, but not sadly so.

I'm still alive. I've learned that sometimes it takes a bunch of small victories to equal an accomplishment. So for now I write...

I write poems for the losers.

I write poems for the lovers and the wretched.

I make jokes for the sad kids to use when they eat lunch with their cool friends.

I probably fall in love 10 times a day with anything around me because the laughter of a child is precious and the way the trees dance with the winds captivates me so.

I know how delicate it all is and I want to take in as much as I can.

The title for this started so very differently,

...and I feel like that's okay really."

Suicide Prevention Hotline

1-800-273-TALK
(8255)

-six words

"whenever you can, give a damn."

-sweet science

left flies out the gate, right observes to win,
left dissects it's way, right protects the grin.
left right's all it's wrongs with speed and callous cause
right left from its perch to reach a crashing halt.
left left right right where it was, left left right home,
right's right where it needs to be while left is gone.
left's the lecture while right is the body.
with left in combo you'll get right to body.
it's Geology, it's the sweetest science.
it's putting honey on a rock and sending it flying.

(this has been intentionally left unfinished and will be continued.)

to find out more about the author visit
www.becauseitsthursday.com

Thank you so much.

rotate.
close.
open.
enjoy.

rotate.
close.
open.
enjoy.

to find out more about the author visit
www.becauseitsthursday.com

Thank you so much.

-The Idea

Maybe because I prayed for her.
Not really in the way you probably just thought of though.
Real prayers. Real words.
I said words from my heart to God's ears
But again, probably not in the way that you're thinking.
I already had her and I prayed for her.
I begged for her, I pleaded.
Almost to the point of tears for her.
Yes, yes I prayed for her.
I prayed that I wouldn't be the man
To break her heart.
I prayed to know what to say to keep her smile.
I probably prayed for something impossible too.
I never thought it would last too long
So I prayed that while it did, I made her happy.
Hell, I tried. I tried like shit.
That's what I hang my hat on.

-Shirts With Pockets

against my face, it's not perfect but that's the all that I have
against my face, place your hand against my face
feel my joy, my pleasure, my pain.
give me amnesty. amnesty from all that I will do.
kiss away the past, and welcome the future.
your kiss tastes of nothing. or at least nothing that I know.
new love. at least for one moment, and one moment again, and
one moment again, but pronounced with pro and proper nouns.
you've already stopped time, you need not worry now, Father
Time himself grows old waiting to begin again.
for one moment again, and one moment again
I hold you. I think of all the times we have been together...
even at initial meeting.
I've met you for the first time again, and my it is magnificent.
as miserly as I am, this love is my food. my drink. my wealth.
for one moment again, I am as a King...please My Love, against
my face. hold your lips against my face.
let not a tear dare dream to peer through your souls windows.
clinch tight now My Love, hold fast your heart and mind.
hold fast my heart as well, it is no longer my own.
for one moment again...
just one moment again I sat in the hallways of love with you and
discussed my truths.
against my heart, though tattered and torn
and badly bruised My Love
against my heart, hold my truths.
against your heart, though tattered and torn
and badly bruised from Love
against your heart, hold my own.

-I Believe In Fears

My footprints left in the sand...
I look back and just before the tide washes
She steps in the same specific places.
I remember how close we were.
I remember how afraid I was.
I remember the look on her face.
I remember how it all felt.
I remember falling in love with her right there on the beach.
Waking before my alarm...
I look over and just at the end of my pillow
She sleeps in almost the same particular space.
I remember how beautiful she was.
I remember how terrified I was.
I remember how long I laid and stared
at the perfection that is her.
I remember falling in love with her right there
moments before my alarm blared for work.
One conversation under the stars about life...
I look over at her because my words escape me.
That's when I see that she catches
the glimmer of hope on my face.
I remember how loud my silence spoke to her.
I remember how frightened her awareness left me.
I remember falling in love with her right there on a cold blanket
under that Virginia sky.
Adjusting the lapel flower of my best man...
I look back and just past the onlooker's smiles and tears
I see her walking towards me one more time.
I remember how bad my anxiety was killing me.
I remember falling in love with her right there in front of
everyone that could see it already.

-Ann Elise

She was my flower and I was deliberate as not to be selfish.
I knew that if I plucked her stem and brought her home
To be admired, that eventually she'd only die.
But that's what she wanted.
That's what she knew. That's what she needed.
She didn't know that she was a flower.
She knew that she wanted to be loved.
She knew that she wanted to be admired.
If it meant that she had to die with me, so be it.
But I was deliberate.
I was careful.
I refused to be selfish.
…and that's how I lost her.

-Mood

Stand up.
Climb.
Climb feverishly out of your boxes.
There are matters at hand that need your fervent attention.
Stop taking guilt trips claiming that your soles hurt.
Opportunity in your hands with you not aware of it's worth.
Generations set free by a compassionate King
And the only thing we're guilty of is having passionless dreams.
The passion, it seems, it flashes, it seems, in splashes, it's seen.
A people obsessed with selfies, yet they're lacking esteem.
Get hot and get steamed.
So often it seems that I'm asked to believe and trust hard
...but even my shadow leaves me alone in the dark.
It gets harder than hard and harder to find things to believe.
With so much strange fruit cut down from my family tree.
Question anything.
Question decisions. Are these solutions?
If there is a question of motive then those questions can ruin.
Question attention, then question intentions and dig deep.
Quick question, is a shepherd still a shepherd without his sheep?
Make success your cologne.
Make sure you reek of revolution.
Make sure your steps are sure and free from pollution.
...and then stand up.
Climb.
Climb feverishly out of your boxes.
...because there are matters at hand that need your attention.

-Her.

Her mind breeds indecision,
Her goals are too far to crawl
This all proceeds inhibitions,
so she'll wait for a star to fall.
Her eyes weep in tradition,
so used to the pain for so long.
So hard to keep Her ambition,
so she settles for things that come.
Her breath is lost with constriction,
she won't put up a fight for more.
Too focused on current conditions,
to know what the fight was for.
Her heart beats with submission,
afraid of the world she knows.
Blood flows from the incision,
some scars just won't heal on their own.
Her soul suffers malnutrition,
so long since she's lost Her self.
She counts her blessings and omissions,
yet Her crown remains on a shelf.
Her hands carry her suspicions,
she's afraid she can't trust all alone.
Afraid she'll bring into fruition,
every fear that she's grown up to own.
Knee deep in intuition,
so sure she'll have no way of escape.
Steadfast in this position,
she thinks that being complacent is safe.
Feet worn from expeditions,
she'll kneel she's in no shape to walk.
Her life's filled with indecision,
so she'll wait for a star to fall.

-Dear Woman,

Do not believe that you are anything less than amazing.
Do not conform.
Do not fold.
Bend if you must, but only at the knee.
Do not set yourself ablaze trying to keep warm this cold world.
You are this world and it lives and breathes through you.
You are the creator of Kings and the ruler of nations.
You are our mothers, sisters, daughters, wives, lovers and
friends, but most of all our equals.
Love yourself, because you come first.
Love your sister, because you know her struggle.
Love us, because you know we need it.
I admire your courage and I envy your resilience.
God bless you.

-one man

-da Vinci's "David"

I can't survive because I'm selfish and I thrive on effort.
Fucking society....but society can't help you perfect your art.
We knew the day would come and as expected we don't last, but
your art only gets better. Your heart may lose a chip, but you
knew that chip needed to go to help perfect your masterpiece...
Your "Atlas."
Your "Christ the Redeemer"
Your "Thinker"
Your heart aches constantly, but you stay the course
because dammit you know what's worse. You know love hurts.
You can see how hurt works.
You just know that you're closer. You just know it's almost over.
You smile because the end is nearer. You can see the outline of
your artwork clearer.
Chip, chip away. Heartbreak, one after the next.
One mans mind and his sex. One step more in your past. It's not
heartache, it's a cast.
So you work and you hurt, and you give up a chip.
Just to lose it because love takes a bit more than this.
Yes, you know what you know but you've made up your mind, that
one day oh one day indeed in due time. You'll complete this piece.
You'll complete your masterpiece and reveal it to the world.
...just like da Vinci, yes, like da Vinci. One day when you're old
and you've lived life a plenty you'll comb through the history
books and you'll revel in the glory of his works.
Then you'll take a step back to admire what you've accomplished.
You'll sit back and realize that through years of chipping away
at your heart through error after error that now you've created a
masterpiece
...a "David".
Yes, just like da Vinci.

-da Vinci's "David"

...it probably weighs on me way more than it should,
but I understand you.
You're an artist, you're amazing and you love to create.
I can see the masterpiece that you're creating with your heart. I
can see the sculpture that you're having created
by all the love and pain that you put your heart through.
You're a good one, you.
No, seriously. I see it now...it's not that you don't want to be hurt,
you expect the hurt. You flourish in the pain, you thrive in it, it
makes you a better you. You know all too well that you couldn't
give me your whole heart, not yet, it's not ready.
That's your masterpiece. You gave your whole heart once and it
got broken, and that's when you started sculpting.
That's what it took, that first chip.
So now you've come up with a plan.
I see it too. I gave you my all, foolish child that I am, I gave you
all that I had and you knew better.
You've learned from the past so you gave me a piece.
You know that if you lose this it only helps create the sculpture so
you know how much you can spare.
We both know you're only hurting us to create art.
Magnificent art.
We both know it'll never work for us this way. I told you that if
you won't give us a real try that it'll never work.
You said you're afraid I'll hurt your whole heart,
but we both know better. You know you'll lose this piece that you
gave me because I can't survive on a piece of you.

I hope for great nights and better days to make one
opportunities are plentiful so I will take one
to pray in the light and let feelings flow from my heart
because even my shadow leaves me alone in the dark.
my ignorance precedes me like a foraging pilgrim
but natures contradiction is my unheralded wisdom.
This definition of success in everything that I address
but unbridled intellect is all that I possess.
I don't wish to be rich. I'd rather live forever in script
Just as quiet as a picture amid unresolved conflict
Relentless intuition, to understand what is missing
is to make full commitment to discard the cards you're given.
She claims to believe in the future, but what does that earn her?
Will she die for her beliefs to be remembered like Nat Turner.
Would you rather be a carbon copy or carved from a rock?
See, I want my words to have power like, say, a Haile Selassie.
...the revolution will be televised, it was narrated by Gil Scott
directed by Spike Lee, and scored by Hip Hop.
starring a man, for names sake we'll call him Tyrone
and systemic belief is that this all begins in my home...

-Be More

...and they're known to leave you hanging
they'll take and take and take
then turn and ask you why you're angry.
I'm just sitting here praying for my brother and his hopes
he's telling me how he would rather riot than revolt.
I know he rambles when he smokes, but I listen to his speech
he says
"apparently it ain't shit for me to get cut down in the street,
and left out in the heat, like strange fruit off a tree.
I'm finding it harder to believe, when the wicked are roaming free
protected by some official that they say was elected by me.
and I refuse to go to school, 'cause dammit college ain't cheap
and my children gotta eat, plus I can't afford the time,
you should know something else,
those history classes don't teach mine,
and if I define cosine it won't help me get hired where I applied,
so if I get killed on my hustle at least I'll die saying I tried."
...and we talked for about two hours.
They can't take away what you've learned,
let that be your super power...

-The Moment

sweat covers my face,
losing my grip on reality the room's still spinning
bass guitars and the snare move me in a way,
now the rhythm is winning
swimming in a tune never heard before,
with a whore that I loved in my dreams
so I wake myself, I was sleeping in love and I don't condone it...
sweating it out

                         lost in the moment

unwrap my eclectic brain from around your finger,
and give me my heart back
unwrap my spaghetti frame from around this glass
and tell me where I parked at
its no door to my soul, I need a jacket,
my hearts bleeding down my sleeve
somebody point me to the door, ready to leave...don't you know it

                    yea I was lost in the moment

-The Moment

wrapping her eclectic brain around my finger,
her heart soon follows.
wrapping her spaghetti frame around the beat,
the liquor's kicked in the door to her soul,
now the world is gone silent and still
motion pictures flowing through her head, she's unaware

> lost in the moment

twist and groove, spinning her web with a level of lies unspoken
with a flick of the hip and a twist of the head,
I see the ending I dread.
didn't know what I was getting into,
now I just know it's not what I want
now I'm up out of my seat, on the dance floor,
on that ass like I own it

> lost in the moment

reading between the lines, I found myself in that single dance
the one between the devil and his mistress,
the one with the sexy stance.
now my world is gone silent and still
motion pictures are in myhead
but I'm so aware, see what I'm doing out here,
I take it as an omen

> lost in the moment

-Blank Canvas

She loved he
and he is me.
and I loved she
for what she never meant to be.
For reasons unseen
She lives in my dreams.
Though I know it's unclean,
I accept it.

-The Last, Last

at your best, be the worst. it is as okay as the sunshine.
write your favorite song with every word you speak.
let every joke be the worst joke you've ever told.
enjoy your beautiful home and family.
cry when that door gets slammed in your face.
write me when times are good...
call me when times are bad...
smile when you think of me.
call when you miss me.

-David the Goliath

The best thing I've ever done was say "I can".
Even meaning it from the heart, I'm a man...
Not excusing myself, but excuse I hold.
Every excuse I spew, excuses grow too old.
So I'm using my tools of screw ups and loose nuts
to bolt to your life and screw up your loose nuts.
To teach you best from my mistakes, that's the best teacher.
I send the memo to you, hoping my excuses reach you.
I'll tell you things like, never follow a woman,
but if she ever needs you, let her know that you're coming...
and never have a regret, and never mess up your credit,
and never ever be violent and never need a cosigner,
and never let em confuse you, and always grow as a student,
and always grow as a person, and love the ones who deserve it,
and if you just get the chance to ever speak on your feelings
don't bottle them bitches in, you'll kill yourself to conceal em.
Keep it real with the real ones, I'm just trying to be real son,
or these words to my daughter, just trying to be a good father.
but be more like your mother, less bad traits that she harbors.
We show you everything bright, but the world is getting darker.
Baby I'm of the world and I'm only trying to reach you,
the world promises you excellence, I just promise to teach you.
I'm just writing from wrong, it's all coming from memories.
Don't bite your tongue till it bleeds,
but close your mouth to your enemies.
There's so much I want to show, and much more I want to tell you.
Don't trust in the unseen except God and the Devil.
Don't you ever worry, I'm David to your Goliaths.
I'll raise you as I can, and watch you grow perfect in silence.

-Greener Pastures

we guess its instilled in the minds of this generation
that feelings must be generated, here's the problem.
she was raised in a project apartment
and from the table of love, she was too early pardoned.
distant and dissed, this just a short list,
very early on in life she was alreadyhardened.
born to a young mother who didn't want her, she gave her cold
shoulders and cut her no slack.
in middle school, new stepdad, he raised her on her back.
high school failed her, she said she's never going back.
moved to one room shack, on the street by the tracks.
flashlights, no heat she would sleep on the floor because its more
to afford a new bed than Jordans.
of course, its a course that you crash in or born in, boring is life
when losing just seems sworn in
black eyes from her boyfriend, who found out how she keeps the
dickcoming in and the money too
no secret what she would do...to afford her Louis Vuitton, Gucci
and Prada couture she was having flown from Cali'
on her feet when she walked the streets she had shoes from Bally
one night left raped in an alley, bruised and beaten badly
next day just as nothing had even happened
fast forward our subject nine months, two sons, no daughter
one's named Jesus because he'll never meet his father
she drops the other off at daycare,
no space there in her one room shack for Jack.
she waits, stares, wipes off fake tears
because she knows that she's never coming back.
she was birthed off luck and then raised off living.
crying to herself because she never got a whipping.
nobody cared...and nobody was there to comfort her soul
when she was down and scared.
ten o'clock news previewed
something that was late breaking...they feared.
no note when she died, just the Savior was there.

-Tokyo Grey

The sounds of the sun kissing earth,
the sounds I hear are't what they once were.
Twice I heard in her the sounds of heaven above,
as good as she looks in nothing, she looks better in love.
She looks better in me, in this mirror on my heart.
...she's heard blue far too long, and she misses
Pleasure...inconsistent but consistent at being just that.
Pleasure, she gives me, so consistent in fact.
She lives in me, deep. Somewhere forgetfulness can't visit,
somewhere I can't reach with a sea of tears...she lives.
...she's tasted red far too long, and she misses
smiles. Far away, but much too close to be seen.
Smiles, she buys from me with cheap jokes.
We'll speak, and I'll swim in her thoughts for years,
bathing in a love this pure, this unformed, this true.
...she's lived black far too long, and she misses
love...but a glance away it is years out of sight.
Love, I hold onto her hold onto me with love.
We wish, we dream, we hope, we pray
because we know where we go we want to stay.
...she's been yellow far too long, and she misses
courage. The bravest of them all but so unsure to try.
Courage. The will in her might die...
but not if I might have my way, I'll love her all my days.
What I see in her is so great. That...
...Tokyo Grey.

-No Working Title

The day is going to come where I no longer
find pleasure in things.
A day will come where I no longer do things for the sake of fun.
A day will come where I'm just merely too old to enjoy life.
On that day I ask, with scrupulous sincerity,
that you will find the most
violently raging river known to man.
When you find this river, my only other request of you is
that you will roll my
casket over into the wildest raging, deepest part.
...I've never been to the rapids.

Bare With Me, I'm Terrible With Names

(excerpt)
by Lian Waite

coming soon...

"Chevron..." she says aloud as she sits dizzily in the now very noticeably chilled bathroom. "...why did I think this much chevron would look good?" she continues aloud while picking at a piece of chipping wallpaper with the same teal and beige chevron pattern as the shower curtain.

In fact, this pattern is repeated on nearly every surface throughout the room. The throw rug and shower curtain, the wallpaper and even the seat cover on the toilet all bare the same pattern. Somehow Maggie was also able to find matching towels, mirror accents and even down to the soap and toothbrush holders. In her inebriated state the designs made the room seem more like a house of mirrors for clowns than a place to relax, so tonight she hurries to finish. After swishing some generic mouthwash around for a moment to clean the remaining vomit residue from her mouth, Maggie turns off the light and heads to bed still mumbling about how much she hates the look of the bathroom.

In the hallway just outside of the bedroom door, she caught a whiff of what she knew would be amplified tenfold once the door was opened, but there was no way around it at this point so in she went.

The pungent and stale air hung heavy with the odor of bodily waste and partially digested mixed vegetables which, in the case of both, were smeared on the wall and bedroom carpet. Turning on the light, she saw the culprits sound asleep, still somewhat in their respective cribs.

Not wanting to wake the children, she just climbs into bed and pulls the covers up almost over her head with plans to clean up the mess in the morning.

Reaching out of the covers she can't seem to locate the light switch to turn off the lamp so she has to pull back the blanket to see where to reach. Out of the corner of her eye she can see that the kitchen light appeared to be on, but she could deal with that in the morning as well.

Maggie manages to pull the string to turn off the lamp and almost an instant later she sees the kitchen light go out.

Maggie slams shut the door, half pissed that she had to go through so much effort to answer the door and half confused because she now wasn't so sure she had ever heard anyone at the door. Just before walking away she recognizes a familiar sound just outside the door, so she opens it again to find that her keys are on the floor just outside of her doorway. Apparently, she left them in the door, and they must have fallen out of the keyhole when she slammed it shut. It's a good thing I found these before someone else did, she thought as she closed the door with a bit less animosity this time.

Tossing the keys on the bookshelf haphazardly, she locks the door and turns her attention to more urgent matters which include changing from her vomit-soaked clothes and getting food and water to help calm the turbulent storm brewing in her stomach.

"The Maggie Way" of getting clean just happens to be throwing a towel over the spot on the floor, stripping off the dirty clothes, tossing them onto the pile and then pulling on the first unstained t-shirt within reach. There was not much of an odor from the incident which, for some odd reason, sat satisfyingly well with Maggie tonight as she moved into the kitchen to search for some type of sustenance to replenish the energy she lost from drinking and the reversal thereof.

In the fridge, she grabs a jar of what is now mostly pickle juice, but there were still two pickles left, so she ate those and drank the half jar of juice before throwing away the empty container. With nothing else cold to drink, Maggie grabs a glass of just cooler than room temperature water from the tap and decides to call it a night.

Making her way to the bathroom for a much-needed pit stop she turns on the light and out of sheer habit closes the door behind her. She notices that when her hand brushes the teal, and beige chevron patterned shower curtain, it flutters just a bit more than usual. Seeing that the window was opened and let in a breeze, she attributes this to the reason that the curtain moves as much as it does and promptly pulls it closed.

Half expecting to hear the wails of pain or whining sounds of needed comfort, she gave a huge sigh of relief because silence was exactly what she, the former doctor, ordered.

Beautiful though it was, her precious silence was short lived because a tremendous pain shot through her gut causing her to bellow out. "UGGGSSHH*T NO NO NO NO NO" she yelled just before collapsing into a ball on the floor.

The combination of too much alcohol, the cigarette and quite possibly her mad dash up the stairs made her vomit once again, but this time all over herself and the carpet instead of into potted shrubbery. She lay there curled in the fetal position for what seemed like a moment, but after coming to and looking at her watch, she saw that it was nearly an hour later.

There seemed to be a knock at the door which awakened her giving her reason to make an attempt at getting up and off the floor. It took a good bit of trying for her to get to her feet and even with help from the bookshelf as mentioned earlier for support, her equilibrium receptors were still going haywire causing her to stumble and fall backward crashing into a small end table before once again collapsing to the floor.

She sat for a moment, dumbfounded and...very drunk, still struggling to maintain consciousness as well as sitting upright when she heard it again. A small tap and then a series of quick knocks at the front door. She was sure of it this time and quickly gathered herself to answer the door. This attempt at standing proved fruitful, and she is able to get to her feet and even grab a nearby towel from the couch and proceed to wipe a bit of the vomit from her face and hands.

She was able to stand up nearly straight, it was her walking however which was very primitive, and it took a moment to make the six or so steps to reach the door.

She swung open the door without so much as a glance out of the   peephole to see who might be knocking at such an hour. To her surprise, there was no one there to be seen. She looked both ways up and down the hall as she leaned against the threshold of the door listening for signs of life, but to no avail. There was not so much as a voice from a television in a neighbors apartment let alone a sound from the culprit who caused the tapping at her door.

It doesn't help that the girl's flailing limbs and shrieks of delight as she is moving to the music intensifies Maggie's nausea while she attempted to survey her surroundings to see if her drinking buddy is watching. He didn't appear to be facing in her direction, so instead of going to the restroom, Maggie made for the exit.

Outside now, in the cooler than comfortable air, wearing the seven shots of tequila as a jacket in place of the real thing and makeup smeared from crying while throwing up, Maggie heads for home. The rapid increase in the liquors effect on her ability to keep standing plus eight or nine blocks of staggering on poorly maintained sidewalks began to make Maggie's six-inch heels start to feel like cinder block boots lined with shards of broken glass. Taking off a shoe and feeling the scores of loose pebbles on the sidewalk she chooses to bear the burden of her beautiful concrete slippers for her final few steps home.

Maggie pulls a two day old, hand-rolled cigarette from her inside coat pocket and lights it to calm her nerves as she's sure there's going to be hell to pay when she walks through the door. A few steps away from her building she notices a neighbor leave the front door of her building ajar and the eagerness to kick off her shoes and make the quick trip up the front steps and into the door overtakes her, and she quickly scoops them up with her free hand as she darts for the entrance.

Up the interior stairs now and walking inside her own apartment with the utmost care to be quieter than a batting eyelash and using the precise foot placement on the squeaky floor like that of a cat burglar she navigates her way inside the second-floor walk-up apartment and eases the front door closed.

Barely able to stand without clenching a nearby bookshelf she looks down at her watch and seeing that it was just after midnight she stands there, lit cigarette still in hand, just inside the door and listens intently to the sounds from inside the home...

Silence...sweet, sultry, beautiful silence.

They must be asleep, finally.

Chapter 1. No Trees

"Why would you let me drink this much tequila?" begged Maggie. "...but we've both had a lot, you must really hate yourself too." She says light-heartedly, looking over to the guy accompanying her for the evening. "My poor bladder is begging me for help right now, so I think I'll make a quick run to the women's room, plus I can feel the shots kicking in already" she laughs. Extending a long, gangling arm, she points to the slew of empty glasses in front of them, "why don't you pay for what we've had so far and the next round is on me, I'll let Lou know."

He nods in agreement as she shoots a quick hand gesture along with a slight nod to Louis the bartender to send one more round of bourbon their way before she staggers off to the restroom. As she slouches through the crowded dance floor Louis solemnly pours the gentleman a shot, he then takes money from his own pocket and puts it in the register and in a mundane and routine sort of way proceeds to clean the newly unoccupied space at the bar.

Maggie is not even halfway across the room when she realizes just how bad of an idea coming out tonight has been. She makes her way through the crowd grabbing onto anyone within reach to keep from falling on her face due to the amount of spinning the room seemed to be doing. Before reaching the bathroom, she finds herself retching into a fake plant just on the other side of the dance floor because her poor stomach is so out of practice for marathon drinking.

She knows she should have just stayed home, but life has been hitting her pretty hard lately and the idea of getting some dupe to buy her free drinks was way too enticing. She gives little effort into pretending to dance with a young lady on the dance floor, but her balance is now more that of an unstable toddler's poor attempt at waddling across its playpen.

Finding
Magdalena Wilder
(excerpt)
by Lian Waite

Dear Reader,

This is a rough, first edit of a story I started a few years ago.
I just wanted to share. I know there needs to be edits.
I know some sentences run on a bit long.
I know the tense is off in certain areas...I know.
I felt like this was something else that I wanted to share.
It'll get a better loving touch before everything is finished.

I also included a few poems from my book
Bare With Me, I'm Terrible With Names.
A few that I liked.
A few that I wanted to share again.
A few that I made a few edits to.

Thank you, enjoy.

LW

to everyone that has been to our acre of "The Creek."

First Printing: 76, G
ISBN 978-0-9966837-9-1

Written, edited & arranged by Lian Waite
All photography & artwork by Lian Waite unless otherwise noted.

This book contains material from
Bare With Me, I'm Terrible With Names (© 2015) by Lian Waite.

Because It's Thursday Publishing
www.becauseitsthursday.com
To contact the author email robert@becauseitsthursday.com

this side up

an incomplete collection of mostly poetry

by Lian Waite

Because It's Thursday Publishing

2019

www.becauseitsthursday.com